This book belongs to

The Duggan Kids. 5

Children's
POOLBEG

TARANTULA!

TARANTULA!

ROSE DOYLE

Children's
POOLBEG

First published 1992 by
Poolbeg Press Ltd
Knocksedan House,
Swords, Co Dublin, Ireland

© Rose Doyle 1992

The moral right of the author has been asserted.

ISBN 1 85371 182 9

A catalogue record for this book is available from the British Library.

Poolbeg Press receives financial assistance from
The Arts Council/An Chomhairle Ealaíon, Dublin

Cover design by Michael Connor
Typeset by Mac Book Limited in ITC Stone 10/14
Printed by The Guernsey Press Company Ltd
Vale, Guernsey, Channel Islands

For Simon and Uriel

Contents

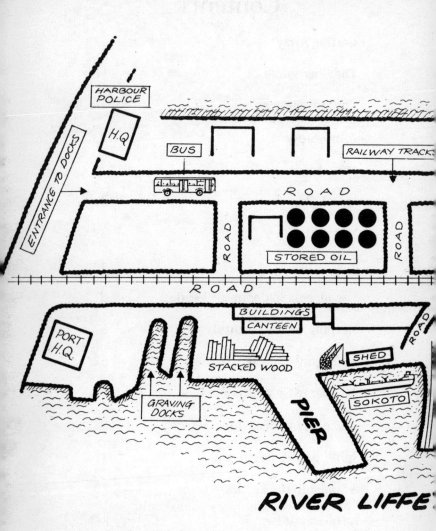

DUBLIN'S DOCKS

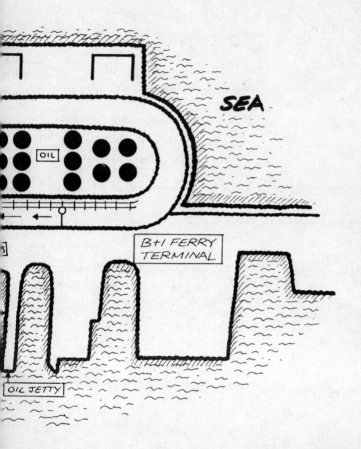

1

Getting Away

It was almost time to go home when Ben and Bobby Kilroy had their brilliant idea. They were sitting on the beach in Sandymount at the time, watching a ship as it came out of Dublin port and moved slowly across the bay. They had been feeling fed up and bored. The idea put an end to all that.

The ship looked like a giant whale. It was, the boys knew, full of people going on holiday. Ben and Bobby had not had a summer holiday. They had spent the whole summer in Sandymount, which was a nice enough place to live but pretty boring when you never got a break.

When the idea came it was so simple they wondered why they hadn't thought of it before.

They would become stowaways. They would stow away on a ship to Liverpool. Their Uncle John, who was a really cool dude and always glad to see them, lived there. They would have the holiday of a lifetime with him. The way their parents had been behaving lately it would probably take them a whole week even to notice they were gone.

"I bet we could do it," said Ben, eyes narrowed as he watched the ship.

"'Course we could," said Bobby impatiently. "Let's get our stuff and go now." Bobby was like that, always wanting to do things immediately.

"No," said Ben decisively, "we'll have to make a plan. It won't work if we don't make a plan."

Ben was ten, a year older than Bobby, which was maybe why he thought about things a bit more. Or maybe it was just the way he was made. He was looking thoughtful now.

"Perhaps we should give Mom and Dad one last chance," he said. "Ask them once more about a holiday. If it's still no, well…"

"Then we're off," said Bobby, who was already half-way there in his mind. They picked themselves up and headed for home. On the way they talked about Uncle John. He was a pilot in Liverpool docks and guided the boats as they came in through the narrower straits of water. He had no children and the boys were his number one mates. He often said so.

"In Liverpool at least we won't have to put up with *her* all the time," Bobby said darkly as they drew near to the house. Home or their parents hadn't been much fun for three months now. Sinéad, their new baby sister, had seen to that. She was a screamer. She cried all day and all night. She was smelly and she took up all their mother's time. She was a real slimer too, splattering milk and baby-food everywhere.

But the truly terrible thing was that she was going to be part of the family for ever and ever and from being a noisy, smelly baby, would grow into a noisy, bossy girl. The boys had liked the family the way it was. Two boys and two parents had seemed to them to be the ideal combination. Bringing in a baby sister had changed everything. If she'd been a baby brother, well, things might have been bearable. But a sister…

Added to all of this was the way their parents seemed not to care about them any longer. Not enough even to take them on a summer holiday. The whole business had filled the boys with a horrible, empty feeling. The sort of feeling you might get if you were told Christmas was finished, never going to come again.

There was nothing to be done about Sinéad. They were stuck with her. They knew that. The holiday was different. They *could* do something about the holiday. That was why, as they watched the ship make its happy, holiday way past the Bailey Lighthouse and on to the horizon, that the brilliant idea of stowing away came to them.

When they got home the house was very quiet. This was most unusual. They stood inside the door and made faces that said "what's up now?" at each other and listened hard. Not a sound. Very strange indeed. Even when the baby wasn't crying their mother was usually fussing about with bottles and clothes and things.

"Must have gone out," Ben shrugged and headed for the kitchen. Their parents had moved the TV in there to amuse Sinéad. The boys had been watching it for what seemed ages when their mother appeared, yawning, in the doorway.

"There you are, boys," she said, beaming at them.

They stared back at her. She hadn't smiled at them for weeks. They weren't going to forgive her *that* easily. She sat down, put an arm around each of them. She hadn't done *that* for weeks either.

"Sinéad's sleeping," she said. "She's been asleep all afternoon. And guess where?"

The boys looked at her warily.

"Where is she?" Bobby asked eventually.

Their mother hugged them. "In the playroom. She seems so happy there. I think we'll convert it into a bedroom for her. You boys won't mind. Will you? You have your own bedroom, after all, and she seems to like it so much there..."

With that their mother got up to make the dinner. Ben and Bobby looked at each other; they didn't have to say a word. Not mind? They minded so much they were speechless. *Their* playroom. Given to *her.* The place where they kept their most precious things. Their racing cars and the train set. The keyboard was in there too, and the drums. It was the only room they could play properly in and make as much noise as they liked. Their bedroom was for sleeping in and was no good at all for playing.

But their bedroom was where they went now to discuss things. They'd have preferred to go to the playroom but of course they couldn't. Not with Sinéad sleeping there.

"Forget about any last chance!" Bobby exploded as soon as they closed the door. "Things are only going to get worse around here."

"You're right," said Ben. He was studying the map of Dublin Port and Docks on their wall. "We'll go tomorrow.

Early in the morning. Let's think up a proper plan..."

They stood and looked at the map. Uncle John had got it for them when he'd brought them on a visit to the docks. The buildings and quaysides were coloured yellow and the river Liffey was a band of blue snaking out into the sea. It helped the boys to remember exactly where everything had been and where they should go to find a ship for Liverpool.

By the time their father got home and called them for dinner they had decided most things.

"We collected some more shells today," Ben said as they sat down. They had decided to say nothing about the playroom. It might arouse suspicions.

"Good. That's great," said their father, who had Sinéad in his arms. "How many hours did you say she slept?" he called to their mother. The boys made faces behind his back. He couldn't fool them. He wasn't a bit interested in what they'd done all day.

"Soon be back at school." Their father turned back, smiling at them. He was feeding Sinéad now. Watching, Ben thought how happy the three of them would be once he and Bobby had gone. They'd probably even be *glad* not to have them around.

The boys behaved immaculately for the rest of the evening. They helped with the wash-up without being asked and went to bed early without an argument.

"Now, let's get on with the rest of the plan," said Ben grimly as soon as they were in their room.

"Right," Bobby agreed, "Let's begin putting it into operation."

They put their savings together and counted them.

£9.43. Not bad. Enough to get there. With any luck Uncle John would be the one to pilot their ship into Liverpool docks. He'd be mighty surprised to find them on board. They would need food too. Bobby liked fruit, especially bananas, so he nipped downstairs and grabbed what fruit he could. This was easy! Sinéad was crying again and nobody heard him. He grabbed some cartons of juice too. Ben produced his secret hoard of chocolate, the one he thought Bobby didn't know about. Ben loved chocolate more than anything in the world. They put the chocolate into Bobby's lunch-box.

Remembering how cold it got at nights they decided to bring their jackets. Finally, they packed everything into Bobby's schoolbag.

They didn't know it then but they were going to be very glad they'd brought Bobby's lunch-box and Ben's jacket.

Packing finished, they discussed a few more details of the plan. Uncle John had brought them into the docks on a number 53A bus and that was how they planned to get in now too. Once inside they would find a ship bound for Liverpool and work out a way to get on board. Remembering the fuss and checking when they'd travelled on a passenger ship with their parents, they decided that a cargo ship was their best hope.

At last, when it was nearly midnight, they got to bed.

Ben didn't sleep at all that night. On the luminous face of the watch he'd been given for his tenth birthday he watched the hours passing, every one. He was sure Bobby must be awake too but when he whispered his name there was no answer. Ben sighed. Bobby was afraid of the dark so he always closed his eyes immediately the lights went out. This of course made him fall asleep very quickly.

The more Ben tried not to think, the more the thoughts came. As the elder he felt responsible for Bobby. He hoped nothing would go wrong—but he was determined that he was not going to back out of things. They had to have a holiday. In two weeks they would be back at school. Everyone in class would be talking about the fantastic times they'd had and the cool places they'd gone during the summer. If he and Bobby didn't stow away they'd have nothing to tell. But if they did…well, then they'd have a brilliant holiday adventure to talk about.

Ben thought and thought as the night went on, wondering if they'd remembered everything. The morning came at last.

Breakfast was the pandemonium it had become since Sinéad arrived—their father rushing about, their mother tired and headachy-looking and the baby, of course, screaming. No one seemed to notice or to care as the boys slipped out the front door and headed off on their summer holiday.

2

The *River Sokoto*

"'Morning lads," said the conductor on the number 3 bus. "How's the form?"

He didn't wait for an answer, just took their money. If he'd waited they'd have told him the form was brilliant. They were sitting in the front seat on the top deck. It was another bright, sunny day and the number 3 was taking them to town, where they would get the number 53A. They had the feeling that a great adventure had begun.

They got off the bus in O'Connell Street and headed for where they remembered getting the 53A. They'd never been in town on their own before and all the time expected someone to stop them, a guard or some adult who knew them, maybe. But no one seemed even to notice them.

They had to sit on the 53A for quite a while before it started off. They didn't mind. Town was a busy place and there was plenty to look at with people of all kinds coming and going. Even so, they were beginning to get a bit anxious when, just before midday, the driver switched the engine into life.

The 53A was a single-decker and everyone was squashed together and friendly. A lot of the passengers were quite sleepy-eyed and you could tell they would have preferred to be at home in their gardens or heading off to the beach. The fat lady who plonked herself down beside the boys, squeezing them against the window, said as much.

"The beach would be nice today, boys, wouldn't it?" she said. She really *was* fat. When she smiled at them her eyes disappeared into the folds of her face. Bobby giggled, imagining her in the water and the gigantic splash she would make. He whispered the idea to Ben, who tried to keep his face straight. It was no good, especially with Bobby giggling away. In a minute the two of them were laughing hard. The fat lady smiled at them again. It was no longer a nice smile.

"Glad to see I'm making someone happy," she said nastily. "And where are you two young men off to, anyway?"

Ben and Bobby looked at one another. The plan hadn't included an answer for adults who might ask them questions before they got to the ship.

"To see our uncle," Bobby blurted out.

Ben said nothing. He was wishing with all his might that he had something—a stinking, smelly sock would have been ideal—to stuff into Bobby's mouth. All he could manage, because of the way they were squashed up, was a warning shove. But the lady seemed to have lost interest anyway.

"That's nice," she said, closing her eyes and seeming to doze off.

Ben glared at Bobby and pinched his arm, hard.

"You're so dumb, Bobby," he said.

"Ouch!" Bobby yelled and managed to elbow Ben in the ribs. "That hurt."

"Stop that, you two," the fat lady had opened her eyes. There was a baleful glint in them now. "I'll have the pair of you put off the bus if you don't stop that carry-on at once," she snapped.

The boys believed her. She was that sort of woman. The sort you knew was always cross with her own children. If she had any. They hoped, if she had, that they were all girls. For the rest of the journey the boys turned their faces to the window and ignored her, pretending not to even notice she was there, heavy and cross in the seat beside them.

When the bus arrived at the gates to the docks they thought, for one heartstopping moment, that they were going to be caught. The harbour police came out of their security box, halted the bus and got on. They looked briskly down the rows of by now hot and sweaty passengers, chatted to the driver and waved the bus on. The boys, breathing easily again but with their hearts beating a bit faster, continued to look steadily out the window.

They'd done it. They were inside the docks.

There were signs everywhere warning of danger, forbidding smoking, naked flames, all sorts of things. As the bus sped along, the boys felt as if they'd left Dublin completely and entered another kind of city. This one had oil terminals instead of office blocks and giant cranes and pipelines where there might have been shops.

And it had ships. They couldn't see them yet but they knew they were there—and that one of them was waiting to take them to Liverpool.

The bus passed thousands and thousands of new cars parked near a huge shed, waiting to be taken away and sold. Then it began to slow down. It rounded a corner and stopped. Everyone got off. Ben and Bobby waited until the fat lady had waddled her grumpy way into a nearby office building, before they too left the bus. From the pavement they stood and watched as it turned and headed back to the city centre.

"We've burnt our boats now," said Ben with a grin.

As jokes went Bobby didn't think it very funny. He was feeling a bit nervous. "We'd better move away from here," he said, "before anyone else asks us where we're going."

Trying not to be too obvious, they took their bearings. This was where they'd got off the bus with Uncle John. They remembered clearly that the quays and the ships were about five minutes' walk to the left. Silently, Bobby pointed. There was a left turning just ahead. Looking as nonchalant as possible, they began walking in that direction.

"I'm hungry," Bobby complained.

"You're always hungry," Ben said, impatiently and with some justification. Bobby *did* like eating.

They turned the corner. In front of them stretched a narrow road with a high brick wall on each side. A lorry was parked half-way down and at the end, sure enough, they could see the quays.

"I'm going to have a banana," said Bobby firmly.

"Oh, all right," said Ben, realising he was a bit hungry himself, "but wait'll we get to the lorry."

Hidden between the lorry and the wall, they devoured a couple of bananas and some of the chocolate, which had become quite mushy by now. They debated eating the rest but decided to keep it—they had no way of knowing how long their food would have to last.

"Right," said Ben, "let's go and look for a ship that's unloading its cargo. When it's empty and the dockers have all gone off we can nip on board and hide. Simple."

"But how will we know which ones stop at Liverpool?" Bobby asked.

"They all stop at Liverpool, dumb dumb."

"Maybe they don't *all*..."

But Ben had moved off. Bobby, with a shrug, followed.

There were no ships docked at the first quay they came to. Carefully, dodging between stacks of timber and the big transit sheds, they made their way to another quay. And there they came upon a huge ship being unloaded. They studied things from behind a container. The activity on the quayside was intense but the most interesting thing of all was the writing on another container waiting to be loaded *on to* the ship. "Destination Liverpool" it read. So it *would* be stopping at Liverpool!

"Just waiting for us," Ben whispered, a small smirk on his face. Bobby didn't argue. He knew it was their ship too. She was enormous. She looked like a huge, dead dinosaur, and almost as old. She was long but fat in the middle where the cargo holds were. Steps wound to the different decks and a green funnel poking the sky had the name *River Sokoto* written on it. Below that they could read Nigeria. An African sailor leant out a window in a big, square section which looked like an apartment block. Other African sailors wandered around the decks. Dockers, using rope slings, were unloading the cargo from the holds. It seemed to be mostly bags of something or other. They were shouting and laughing as they worked, using a lot of words which would have got them into terrible trouble with Ms Bateman, the boys' teacher. The arms of a colossal crane were lifting the bags on to lorries. The lorries left as soon as they were full up.

"An African ship!" Bobby breathed.

Ben nodded.

"It looks pretty rusty," he said.

"Probably from the sun," said Bobby.

"A venerable vessel," Ben said, showing off, though it wasn't clear to whom, since Bobby ignored him when he used big words. Neither of them cared about the rust, nor about how old the *River Sokoto* was. She was their kind of ship.

As they risked moving a bit closer, a crunching sound, followed by a familiar smell, made them look down. They had stepped on some small, brown beans. The smell was familiar because it was of chocolate. It came from the powder inside the beans.

Ben wet his finger and tasted the powder. It was bitter but definitely chocolaty.

"Cacao beans." His eyes had become very bright. "That's what they're taking off the ship. Cacao beans! For making chocolate!"

Then, before Bobby realised what he was doing, Ben had dropped to his knees and was crawling toward a pile of spilled beans. He'd gone several feet before Bobby was able to catch his foot and drag him back. But it was too late. They'd been spotted.

"Hey!" shouted a docker, "what're you kids doing here?"

In a flash, both boys were on their feet and running, as if wild dogs were after them. They could hear the shouts of other dockers but didn't look back. They just kept running until they reached the stacked timber and found a place to hide.

"That was a dopey thing to do!" Bobby hissed. "You could have ruined everything over some old chocolate beans. You can't even eat them, you know."

"Yes you can," whispered Ben though, now that he thought of it, he realised that sort of concentrated chocolate could be very sickening, even for a stomach as used to chocolate as his.

They heard running feet coming closer and held their breath. They didn't dare look out when two sets of legs stopped right beside them.

"Must have been somebody's kids brought in to see the docks," said the voice of the man who'd yelled at them.

"Yeah," said a second man. "You're probably right. They'd never get in here otherwise."

The men moved off. The boys waited for what seemed forever before venturing out and making their careful way back to the ship.

When they got there the dockers had gone and both the quayside and ship seemed very quiet. From the side of a transit shed the boys studied the scene carefully.

"It's too early to go on board," said Ben. "We'd better hide in this shed until it gets dark."

Quickly and silently they slipped from the side to the front of the shed and through the half-open door. Near the back there were some cacao bags and they sat down to rest, leaning against them and feeling safely out of sight. They could see the *River Sokoto* from there. She still looked very impressive.

3

The Stowaway

The boys settled down to wait. It was very hot in the shed and the smell from the bags and from some crushed beans on the floor made them feel they were in a chocolate factory. Ben closed his eyes and pretended he'd arrived in heaven. A fairly dingy, gloomy heaven. But heaven must smell like this, he reckoned. The only light came from the half-open door. Apart from the cacao bags, a fork-lift truck and a couple of small containers, the shed was empty.

"It's gross," said Bobby, holding his nose. "I'll get sick if I stay around this smell. I'm going to wait in that fork-lift."

"Please yourself," said Ben, "but be careful you don't make any noise."

"Be careful yourself," muttered Bobby as he headed for the fork-lift and climbed into the cab. He felt good in there, pretending to drive it away from the chocolate smell and making engine noises.

Leaning against the bags Ben began to feel sleepy. After all, he hadn't slept the night before. He felt as if the world of mothers and fathers, families and schools was a million miles away. The bags looked inviting. A snooze on a chocolate bed was just what he needed. He lay across the bags and closed his eyes. It wasn't as comfortable as he'd hoped but he began to doze anyway. He was almost asleep when he felt the bags move.

"Watch it, Bobby," he said, annoyed.

"What do you mean, watch it?" Bobby's voice came from the fork-lift across the shed. Must have been dreaming, Ben thought. Then he felt the bags move again. A sort of wriggling movement, right under him.

Ben was sensible some of the time. Cacao beans, he knew, could not move like that. As if they were solid and alive. On account of his interest in chocolate he knew all about cacao beans. He knew they grew on the cacao tree and that they were hacked down by machetes while still in their pods. That they were then taken out of the pods, dried in the sun, packed into bags and sent around the world to be made into chocolate. Nothing he'd ever read said anything about the beans being able to move.

So—there must be something else in the bags. Or in one bag at least. He could feel the wriggling again and now he could tell that it came from one bag only. His heart began to hammer. It could be anything. Some wild jungle animal, maybe, which had slept all the way from Africa and had now woken up and was trying to get free. He held his breath and lay very still. He could hear Bobby making his pretend driving noises on the fork-lift. He wished he would shut up but was too scared to yell at him.

Fearfully, Ben let his breath out again. The wriggling still went on. What if it was a snake? Africa was full of snakes.

A python or cobra or boa constrictor could easily have slithered into one of the bags when they were being packed in Africa. Ben's mouth went quite dry. He knew he would have to get away from the bags. He couldn't just lie there and wait to be bitten. And die. He would have to get off the bags without attracting the thing's attention.

Ben took a deep breath and began to slide slowly. At first it seemed he was going to make it but then he felt himself losing his grip. Frantically he tried to hold on but it was no good. With a crash, he fell to the ground, one of the bags falling with him. Numb with horror, he watched as it began to wriggle across the shed toward the door.

He could hear Bobby making gasping sounds and knew that he'd seen the wriggling bag too. For what seemed like eternity the boys watched the bag make its way toward the door. Then it stopped. Just stopped still and lay there. It was a very lumpy-looking bag—big lumps. It very definitely did not contain beans.

High on the fork-lift Bobby felt a little more confident. The best thing, he thought, would be to throw something at the bag and see what happened. There were some lengths of wood on the cab floor and he lifted one, took careful aim and threw it. Bull's-eye! Right in the centre of the bag! What happened next was astonishing. The bag yelled. A loud, very human yell. Then it began to wriggle toward the door again, faster than before.

But the boys weren't half as frightened now. The yell had told them what they needed to know. There was a person in the bag. A not very big person either, and one who was afraid of them. Otherwise, why would he be trying to get away? Bobby climbed down and together, very slowly, he and Ben went after the bag. It was nearly at the door now.

"Right!" Bobby hissed. "Let's get it!"

They pounced, grabbing a corner each. The bag really began to yell then. It began to kick too, and to thrash about in a most amazing way. The boys could hardly hold on.

"If we let you go," Ben called, "will you come out quietly?"

A muffled sound came from inside the bag.

"I think it said yes," said Bobby, who didn't think so at all but had just been given a terrific kick by the bag. He let go and so did Ben. For a few seconds nothing happened. Then, just as the boys were about to pounce on it again, the top of the bag began to open.

At first the boys thought a mound of cacao beans was trying to get out. Then they saw that it was hair; thick, curly black hair. They watched, speechless, as a pair of black eyes followed the hair and then, very slowly, the whole of an African girl about their own age climbed out of the bag. She was dark brown and wore a skirt and tee-shirt. She pulled two brightly coloured blankets out of the bag with her and stood looking at the boys, eyes fiercely glittering.

Bobby was the first to find his voice.

"Who're you?" he asked.

"Who're you?" the girl replied.

"She probably doesn't speak English," Ben said.

"Of course I speak English!" the girl said in an annoyed

voice. "Everyone in Nigeria speaks English."

"You're from Nigeria?" Bobby asked.

"In Africa?" Ben echoed. They could hardly believe their ears. She looked African enough—but could she really have come all that way? And in a cacao bag by the looks of things.

"Yes. Nigeria in Africa," the girl said. "I came from Lagos on the *River Sokoto*. I'm a stowaway." She sounded very proud of herself.

"You're a *stowaway*?" This time the boys echoed together. The girl looked annoyed again.

"Why do you keep saying everything after me? Yes. I stowed away. It was easy, except for the last bit when I had to get off the ship this morning. That was horrible. I've still got some bruises—and you two pulling me about in the bag didn't help things."

"We didn't know it was you," Ben protested. "You should have said something."

The girl put a blanket around her shoulders. "Is it always so cold in Dublin?" she asked. The boys felt a bit insulted.

"It's warm today," Ben said but then, remembering where she'd come from, added, "though I suppose it's not so hot as Africa."

"Why did you stow away?" Bobby asked. He was feeling a bit peeved that a mere girl should have stowed away, and so successfully, all the way from Nigeria.

"Because I wanted to get away from my family." The girl seemed very matter-of-fact. "I bet my mother and father are good and worried about me by now."

"Don't you care?" Bobby asked. She sounded very

brave and cool but you never could tell. It had occurred to Bobby that his own parents might be worried by now. He didn't want to think about it.

"They don't care about me any more," the girl said. "They want to move the family from Lagos. My mother says it's too crowded. They want to live in Ibadan. But all my friends are in Lagos and so is my school and everything. They didn't even ask me. They just decided. So *I* decided I wasn't going with them."

She went all quiet then and stood looking at the ground. She seemed pretty fed up. For a horrifying moment the boys thought she was going to cry.

"That's pretty brave," said Ben, hoping the compliment would cheer her up. It did. She looked at him, decided he was being nice and tried a grin which nearly worked. Then she began to look around the shed.

The boys raised their eyebrows at each other. It was a sign which said "can we trust her?" She *seemed all right* but it was better to be sure. She could be a spy. They'd heard of foreign countries using children as spies. On the other hand if she wasn't a spy, she could tell them all sorts of things they needed to know about the *River Sokoto*.

"What's your name?" Ben asked, sternly.

"Zabeth. But everyone calls me Zaby. You can if you like," said the girl.

"We're called..." Bobby stopped when he saw the ferocious face Ben was making at him.

"Not yet," he said to Bobby and turned to Zaby. "Have you ever seen a lion? Or a giraffe or a tiger?" This was a trick question. He meant to test her.

"Of course I've seen lions. And giraffes. The National Parks in Nigeria are full of them. But there are no tigers in Africa. Don't you know *anything*?"

"It was a trick question. Of course I know." Ben felt a bit silly. He knew she didn't believe him. She thought he was stupid.

"If you're really a stowaway tell us how you got on the ship and how you got off," Bobby demanded. These were the things he and Ben needed to know.

"All right," Zaby moved back to the bags and sat on them, "but only if you give me something to eat first. My tummy feels really empty."

Ben gave her some chocolate, making a big deal of it, of course. Bobby gave her a banana and Zaby began to tell her story.

4

Zaby's Story

"Getting to the docks was the easy bit," said Zaby. "I just took a bus." The boys could believe that all right. "When I got there it was getting dark and there were millions of people about. There are a hundred million people in my country you know. It's the most important country in Africa..." But Zaby could see from the impatient looks on the boys' faces that they didn't want to hear about Nigeria. She went on with her story. "Anyway, with all those crowds about it was easy to slip in where the ships were."

"How did you find one bound for Dublin?" Ben wanted to know.

"That was an accident," said Zaby. "I saw men loading those beer modules." She pointed to where two stood on the quay outside. "They had Guinness, Dublin written on them and I thought it sounded like a faraway enough place to go. When no one was about I climbed up the anchor chain and on to the deck." Zaby shivered a bit, remembering. "It swung a bit from side to side as I went up. But it's a very big chain so I wasn't really worried."

Bobby gulped. He didn't like heights and an anchor chain, swinging high above the waters of the Liffey, sounded a terrifying way to get onto the *River Sokoto*. Zaby was still talking.

"I sneaked all over the ship and when I came to that lifeboat—" she pointed again and the boys, following her finger, saw a very solid-looking lifeboat near the top deck of the *River Sokoto*, "I climbed inside and hid under the tarpaulin."

The boys were impressed—not that they allowed Zaby to see this of course. Ben wondered if all African girls were like her.

"Finding the lifeboat was a real piece of luck," Zaby went on, "because I'd forgotten to bring food with me." The boys smirked to themselves when she said this. *They* would never be so dumb as to forget to bring food. "But the lifeboat was stocked with sea rations so I got food anyway. There was chocolate, even—and water of course." Their smirks faded. Zaby was obviously a very lucky person.

"The lifeboat was right beside the sailors' sleeping quarters so I could hear them coming and going and I didn't feel so lonely. I made a hole in the tarpaulin so I could peep out. There's a swimming pool up there too—," the boys really perked up at this "—but it's empty,"—and dashed all their hopes of secret night-time swims. "It was nice on the lifeboat, except that..." Zaby stopped, as if gathering thoughts in her head.

"Don't leave anything out," Ben warned and, to make sure she wouldn't, gave her another piece of chocolate.

"Well," Zaby munched, "it was kind of spooky at

night. Very whispery and terribly dark. There were creaking noises, too, from the masts and the doors and even the lifeboat. The sea went pitch black and sort of swelled up. It was like being on the back of a huge, groaning animal." Zaby took a deep breath. "I didn't like it very much so I decided to sleep somewhere else."

"Early one morning, just after all the sailors got up, I had a look around and found some empty cabins. I chose the least smelly one and moved in there. I still spent the days on the lifeboat so as I could peep out and see what was going on."

The boys were beginning to feel pretty good about things. Theirs would be a short, daytime journey and they wouldn't have the problem of spooky nights. Everything sounded quite easy. Anyway, if a girl could make it all the way from Africa, they could stow away as far as Liverpool. But there were still some things they needed to know.

"Tell us how you got off when you got here," Bobby asked, "and how you got into the bag."

"That," Zaby shivered, "was the worst part. Very early this morning, just after it docked, the ship was searched. I was in the lifeboat so I could see everything. There were crowds of police and customs men and they sent dogs sniffing around the cargo holds. My heart was really hammering. I was so scared the dogs would smell *me*. If I'd been caught then they'd have sent me straight back to Nigeria. That's what they do with stowaways, you know. They send them straight back to the country they come from."

The boys hadn't known this but in truth they were a

bit relieved to hear it. Being sent back was a lot better than being sent to jail, which was what they had supposed happened.

"The dogs didn't smell me of course," Zaby said, "but when they went away the other men came and began to unload everything. I was pretty worried by then because I didn't know how I was going to get off. There were men everywhere, putting the cacao bags into rope slings and then getting the big cranes to lift them into lorries."

The boys remembered seeing all of this. Zaby pointed through the door again. One of the cranes, an absolutely gigantic one, was still outside.

"We saw all of that too," Bobby said, rather grandly. "So how did you get off? And how come you're here in the shed and not gone off in a lorry?"

"I'm lucky to be in a shed," Zaby snapped. "I was nearly killed. I bet neither of you could do what I did..."

"Oh yes, we could," Bobby cried.

"Tell us what you did and we'll see," said Ben, who was usually a bit more cautious than Bobby.

"Well," Zaby ignored Bobby and spoke directly to Ben. "While I was wondering what to do two men came and stood by the lifeboat. Right beside where I was. I couldn't see their faces but I could see their arms and hands through my peephole." There was a quiver in Zaby's voice now. "One of them was Nigerian but the other was from Dublin. He was the really bad one. He sounded evil and cruel. His hands were gruesome: big, hairy-looking things. The sailor called him Murt."

The boys couldn't help wondering if Zaby was exaggerating a bit here, trying to impress them. "What were they talking about?" Ben asked, and both boys watched Zaby closely as she replied.

"About smuggling drugs," said Zaby and paused to see what the boys thought of this. Their faces showed clearly that they didn't believe her.

"They *were*! " Zaby insisted, then stopped talking. She looked quite hurt.

"Well, tell us," Bobby coaxed.

"Why should I?" Zaby asked huffily, "if you're not going to believe me. Anyway, you haven't even told me your names."

"All right," said Ben, pointing at his brother. "He's Bobby and I'm Ben. And we believe you. Now tell us..."

"Well..." Zaby didn't look convinced but she told them anyway. "The one called Murt kept talking about some special bags. He was blaming the sailor for getting them mixed up with the others but the sailor said if he hadn't, the dogs would have found them. Then Murt said he'd have to get them off the ship quickly and into this shed. They moved away after that and I saw their backs. Murt looked very square and tough. Even his head was square."

"So what happened about the special bags?" Ben was developing an uneasy feeling about the pile Zaby was sitting on.

"Well," said Zaby, "all the men went off on their break then. There was nobody about so I climbed down to the hold they were unloading the bags from..."

"And you got into one?" Bobby guessed.

"Yes. It was the only way I could think to get myself taken off."

"I emptied one out," Zaby giggled, "then I wrapped myself in my blankets, got inside and held the top closed." She looked at the boys with huge eyes. "I was nearly killed when they lifted me up with the other bags. I could feel the ropes tightening around me and the other bags squashing me and I couldn't breathe. It was like being picked up and squeezed in a giant's hand. I was swung through the air and, just when I thought I was really going to die, the crane caught the bags and dumped them on the quayside. That was *really* sore," Zaby rubbed her bottom, "but my blankets saved me a bit. Murt came along then and lifted the pile onto a fork-lift and brought it in here." She bounced a little on the bags. "The drugs they were talking about are somewhere in this pile."

5

Murt Arrives

All three of them looked closely at the pile of beans. Then they poked them. They *felt* like cacao beans. Ben helped himself to a few from a loosely closed bag and cracked them between his teeth. They tasted like cacao beans too.

"I dunno," he grinned, "they all seem full of beans to me."

Bobby grinned too. Zaby didn't think it much of a joke.

"Some of them *must* have drugs in them," she argued, "and I bet Murt will be coming back for them. I don't want to be here when he does."

She began to wander around the shed, examining everything. Bobby counted the bags. There were nine, not counting the one Zaby had been in.

"Nothing much here." Zaby had completed her tour. "I'm going to slip away tonight. As soon as it gets dark."

"Where will you go?" Ben asked. Zaby made a face at him.

"Mind your own business," she said. But from the way she said it Ben somehow knew she had no idea where she was going to.

"Do you know anybody in Dublin?" he asked, though he knew the answer to this too.

"No." Zaby came and stood directly in front of him. "But now I know you two. You can help me get out of here and tell me where to go."

"No, we can't!" Bobby spoke loudly so that Zaby would know he meant it.

"Why not?" She looked puzzled. "If you were in Nigeria I would help you."

"Because we're going to stow away ourselves tonight."

For the second time that day Ben felt like stuffing something in his brother's mouth. Only it was too late now. Zaby was looking *very* interested. If she really was a spy, and he still half believed she was, then she would definitely betray them now.

"Where are you going?" Zaby's question seemed natural enough. Bobby, ignoring the thunderous look on Ben's face, told her they were going to Liverpool.

"Can I come with you?" Zaby asked at once. The boys were shocked.

"No," said Bobby, "we're going to our uncle. He wouldn't like it if we turned up with a strange girl."

"Strange?" Zaby looked furious. "What do you mean *strange*? You're strange yourselves, hanging around this old shed like a pair of cockroaches." She gave them a withering and superior look. "I suppose you intend stowing away on the *River Sokoto*?"

"Why shouldn't we?" Ben could feel his face burn with annoyance.

"Because the *River Sokoto* is going to be here for another day, that's why. They'll be cleaning and loading it up and doing all sorts of things and you'll be caught if you go on board tonight. That's why."

The boys thought about this. If she was right, and they somehow thought she was, then it was very bad news indeed. They certainly could not hide in the shed until tomorrow night. They were sure to be caught long before then.

"I could help you find another ship," said Zaby, sounding like someone who had spent a lifetime stowing away, "but why do you *want* to stow away?"

The boys looked at her, hard. They could see now that she had a cut on her arm and what looked like a bruise on her cheek. She had a sort of pleading expression on her face, as if she really wanted to be friends.

"What age are you?" Ben asked.

"Ten and a half," Zaby answered. Her voice had got smaller.

"And you're not a spy?"

"Of course I'm not a spy!" Indignation made Zaby's voice strong again.

So the boys told her all about Sinéad and how their parents didn't care about them any longer either and how they were going off to Uncle John, who did. Zaby didn't interrupt once while they were talking.

"Doesn't sound too bad to me," she said when they were finished. "At least they didn't try to take you away from your friends and school and everything."

"Who knows what they'll try to do next," said Bobby darkly, "now that they've given her our playroom."

"If we go to Liverpool," said Zaby, "I won't get a chance to see Dublin. What's it like? Are there many people living here?"

"Thousands," said Bobby.

"Thousands and thousands," said Ben.

"I'll bet there aren't as many as in Lagos," said Zaby. "Where do you live?"

"Across the river." Ben waved an arm towards the Liffey outside, "and out a bit. It's not far, really."

"Is the river big?" Zaby walked over to the door and looked out.

"It's big all right," said Ben. "It's called the Liffey. It's very famous, too. Have you never heard of it?" He was remembering the tigers and how she'd made him look silly.

"Nope," said Zaby cheerfully, "never heard of it." She was trying to slide open the door. It was very stiff and she was making a lot of noise. "It's not as famous as the river Niger anyway—and I bet it's not as long. The Niger is 2,600 miles long."

The boys found this hard to believe. Could any river be *that* long? While they thought about it, Zaby succeeded in opening the door a little wider.

"Hey," she called. "It looks nice out there. No people. Amazing. I can see an island further out too. How long is the river?"

"That's not an island," said Bobby, "that's Howth. And the Liffey is 83 miles long." He'd chosen a study of the Liffey for his project in school last month. He knew how very useful, and beautiful, a short river could be. How it could be of much more value than anything 2,600 miles long. He remembered something else.

"It comes from the Wicklow mountains," he added.

"It would be nice to see more of it while I'm here,"

Zaby said, rather grandly, Bobby thought.

"Someone will see you if you don't come away from that door," called Ben, who wasn't wild about Zaby's attitude to the Liffey either. She closed the door over again and came immediately to sit cross-legged on the bags beside them.

"Tell me about Dublin," she said eagerly.

Together the boys began telling her things they thought would interest her. They told her about their school and their friends. About the swimming pool they went to and the parks where they played football and about Sandymount beach. Then Zaby told them about Lagos, which sounded bigger than Dublin and an awful lot hotter. They asked her about the National Parks and she told them about the huge African bush elephants she'd seen there.

"What colour is Nigeria's flag?" asked Bobby. He was quite into flags.

"Green, white and green," said Zaby.

"Nearly like ours..." Bobby stopped short as a grating noise at the shed door made the three of them jump. There was a man outside, a man whose outline looked very square against the bright light. He was opening the door wider to let himself in.

Silent as cats the children slipped down behind the bags and like cats they curled themselves into small balls. They could hear the man coming into the shed.

There was silence then, except for a short cracking sound. Ben risked a quick peep. The man had struck a match and was lighting a cigarette. His fingers were big and hairy-looking...

Ben ducked down. Beside him he could feel Zaby shaking. When he looked at her he saw that her eyes had become round and large with fear. She gripped his arm, squeezing it so hard it hurt. He would have yelled only he was afraid to.

"That's him," she whispered. "That's Murt, the man from the ship. He must have come for his bags of drugs..."

6

It's a Killer!

Murt moved into the shed and stood in the gloom inside the door. He seemed to be watching the ship. He really was square, just as Zaby had said he was. Even his head was square. It merged into his huge shoulders as if he had no neck at all.

The children could see the tip of his cigarette glowing red every time he pulled on it. When he came to the end he ground the butt under his foot and immediately lit another. He seemed very nervous. He was half-way through the second cigarette when hurrying footsteps stopped outside the shed and a Nigerian sailor slipped through the door.

"You took your time getting here." Murt's voice was as nasty as Zaby had said it was. It had an edge like a rusty, poisonous razor blade. Ben and Bobby cringed, but inwardly, so that Zaby couldn't see. Listening to that voice you could believe everything she had said.

"I had to be sure no one saw me." The sailor's voice was low.

"I hope no one did!" Murt snarled, "for all our sakes. If things go wrong at this stage it'll be—" he made a sinister strangling sound and drew a finger in a cutting motion across his neck "—for all of us. The Boss'll…"

"I know what the Boss will do—" the sailor interrupted, his voice rising "—but nobody saw me, I tell you…"

"Keep it down, keep it down," said Murt, lowering his own voice. "Walls have ears and you never know who might be listening."

The children caught their breaths. He couldn't possibly know they were in the shed, could he? He was lighting another cigarette as he spoke and he certainly wasn't looking in their direction.

"Careful with the cigarettes in here," said the sailor. And Murt laughed. It was not a nice sound.

"I'll be on cigars for the rest of my life when this deal goes through," he said, "and I won't be smoking them in transit sheds in Dublin docks either."

"All right, all right." The sailor sounded worried. "I have to get back to the ship, so here's the position. I met our friend and told him where the bags are. You're to meet him at 5.15 p.m. in the dockers' canteen. He's not pleased about the delay…"

"He'd be feeling a lot worse if the dogs had sniffed out the stuff this morning," Murt growled. Turning, he looked right across at the children's hiding place.

Bobby felt his heart turn right over as Murt started to walk toward them. He crossed his fingers and closed his eyes. Murt stopped right in front of the bags.

"They'll be safe enough here for the time being," he said. "No one's going to move them tonight."

"Not while I'm on watch, anyway," said the sailor. Ben and Zaby could see the men's faces now. It was difficult in the gloom to make out the sailor's brown face but Murt's looked as if it had been made out of lego. Everything about it, except for his small, mean-looking eyes, was square.

Then, as they watched, his face took on an expression of petrified fear. His mouth began to open and close but no sounds came out. He lifted a trembling hand and pointed to the bags.

"Kill it!" His voice, when he managed at last to get it out, came in a thin, squealing sound. "Kill it! Kill it!" Bobby opened his eyes just as the sailor caught Murt roughly by the arm.

"Control yourself, man," he snapped. "It won't touch you if it's left alone." He tried to pull Murt with him toward the door but Murt seemed rooted to the spot, his eyes fixed on the bags.

"It's a killer," he said in the same squeaky, terrified voice.

"Don't be a fool," said the sailor. "Do you want to screw everything up because of—look, it's gone. Come on, let's get out of here."

Murt seemed to recover some of his angry snorting as he allowed himself to be propelled out of the shed.

"It'll be a fork-lift job when I come back for those bags," he said. "I'm not going to touch them. Not with that thing in there…"

The children, relieved but shocked and fearful too of whatever it was that had frightened Murt, relaxed a bit. They didn't breathe freely until the men's voices, and then their footsteps, had faded along the quayside. But it wasn't until there was complete silence, except of course for the cries of the gulls and some church bells ringing across the river, that they dared leave their hiding place. They stretched the stiffness out of their bodies and Bobby uncrossed his fingers.

"Wow!" he said. "I thought we were dead meat for sure..."

"They're real scumbags all right," said Ben.

"What're scumbags?" Zaby asked.

"Scumbags? Don't you know what scumbags are? They're really bad types who rob and beat people up and stuff," Bobby explained.

"I think we need a plan," said Ben thoughtfully. "We'll have to have a think about all of this. Things are really changing around here."

7

Into Action

No one wanted to sit on the bags so they all clambered up into the cab of the fork-lift. Ben pulled the door tightly shut after them. They were a bit squashed but they felt safer there, both from unwelcome visitors and whatever was creeping around the bags.

"I wonder what frightened Murt like that?" Zaby said. "Maybe we should have a look."

"Probably a rat," said Ben. "Lots of people are terrified of rats. It's probably still there, too."

"Better to find out what it is if we're going to spend the night here," said Zaby.

Cautiously, they got down from the fork-lift. Just as cautiously they searched around the bags Murt had pointed to. They even aimed a few kicks at them. Nothing moved; no rat scurried away.

"Who says we're going to spend the night here?" Bobby asked. The shed didn't seem so appealing any more.

"That's what we need to discuss," said Ben. "Whatever happens we're in this together now. We're the only ones who know what those rotten smugglers are up to—so we're the ones who'll have to stop them. We'll have to come up with a plan..."

Bobby heaved a sigh. He wished Ben wouldn't make such a big deal about thinking all the time. But he lay back and listened anyway. Zaby was leaning against the perspex window of the cab and looking at the bags on the ground below. Bobby felt sure she wasn't listening.

"Question is," Ben said, "how do we stop them without giving ourselves away?"

Bobby looked at him blankly and Zaby, who must have been listening after all, turned around looking puzzled. What *did* he mean?

"Look." Ben spoke as if he was dealing with two infants. "If they see us then it's no Liverpool or Uncle John for you and me, Bobby, and—" he turned to Zaby "—it's back to Nigeria on the boat with you, Zaby. Understand, dumbos?"

"Dumbo yourself," said Bobby automatically. He thought about what his brother had said. Ben was right, of course. They would have to destroy the scumbags' smuggling plan with great cunning and secrecy and without being seen themselves.

"So," said Ben, "what do we know?"

"That Murt is meeting someone in the dockers' canteen at 5.15 p.m.," said Bobby. "And we know where that is too. Uncle John brought us there, remember?"

"Yes." Ben was looking thoughtful again. "They'll be making plans then to get the bags out of here. One of us will have to go along and listen. That'll be the first part of the plan..."

"I'll go," said Zaby eagerly. "You tell me where this canteen place is and I'll go..."

"You can't!" said Bobby and both boys looked at her, shaking their heads.

"Just because I'm a girl," Zaby began, indignantly.

"It's *not* because you're a girl," said Ben. "It's because you're African. Everyone would notice you. You look too different…"

"There are hardly any African girls in Dublin," Bobby explained. "You wouldn't get anywhere near Murt without everyone looking at you. Anyway, Murt would be sure to suspect something as soon as he saw an African girl…"

Zaby looked from one to the other of the boys. She seemed to be thinking about what they had said. Eventually she nodded. "Well," she said, "what time is it now?"

Ben checked his watch. He was amazed to see they'd been more than four hours in the docks already.

"It's five past five," he said. "Someone had better go pretty soon…"

"I'll go," said Bobby. "I'm dead thirsty anyway so I'll get myself a drink and sit near them. That way I'll hear their plans."

"No. I'll go," said Ben firmly. "You'd start talking to Murt or something dopey like that…"

"I would not!" Bobby yelled, really angry. "I'm not stupid, you know."

He had opened the cab door and was beginning to climb out of the fork-lift when Zaby put out a hand to stop him.

"Wait," she said, "I've been thinking too." She was grinning. "Why don't you toss a coin to see who goes? Look, use this Nigerian coin. It's called a naira."

Bobby stopped and the boys looked at her, then at the coin in her hand.

"Okay," they said together.

"Right then." Zaby became very businesslike. "Heads Bobby goes, tails it's Ben." She spun the coin expertly in the air, caught it deftly in her palm as it came down then turned it on to the back of her hand.

"It's tails," she announced.

"Well, that's that," said Ben. "I'll take some money with me and get us something to drink while I'm there. And something to eat."

"I don't want chocolate," said Bobby. He felt he never ever wanted to eat chocolate again. Ben took some money and began to climb down from the fork-lift.

"Be careful." Zaby warned. "That Murt's a real scumbag..."

Ben grinned. Zaby was a fast learner. But he was a bit embarrassed too.

"'Course I'll be careful," he said, "and you two be careful as well. Stay out of sight, don't go outside. And Bobby—if anyone comes into the shed *don't talk* to them. Stay hidden. If you give us away you're history..."

With that he was gone, slipping quietly through the gap in the door.

"What does he mean, you're history?" Zaby asked.

"He's just trying to frighten me," Bobby shrugged. "He likes to sound tough. But he's not. I'm tougher than he is..."

Zaby sighed, the sort of sigh which said "I've heard all of this before." Then she sat on the floor of the cab, with one blanket under her and the other wrapped around her. In a moment she was asleep and gently snoring.

Bobby, just for one sharp moment, thought of his bed at home, of his quilt with the motorbikes on it that his mother had allowed him to choose for himself. She'd be worried about him and Ben by now, probably looking everywhere. Maybe even crying...

He put the picture of their mother crying out of his head. She had Sinéad. Most likely she wasn't worried about them at all.

He sat in the driver's seat and ate a banana. It was the last. He hoped Ben wouldn't be too long. He hated waiting and he was still hungry. Then he began pretending to drive the fork-lift again.

8

Spy Tactics

Ben, blinking hard, stood outside the door of the shed for a few seconds. Slowly, as his eyes adjusted to the light, the spots disappeared from in front of them. He started for the canteen then, moving carefully and making sure no one saw him. This wasn't difficult since there were few people about.

He remembered exactly what the canteen looked like. It was a square grey building with high windows and a red door. He was also sure that he remembered where it was, but twice, just when he thought he'd found it, the building turned out to be something else. It was 5.10 on his watch. He tried not to panic but knew he had to find the canteen soon. What if Murt and the man he was meeting left the canteen, went somewhere else? He'd never know then what their plans were. Or supposing they decided to go to the transit shed straight away? He'd never be able to warn Bobby and Zaby.

Ben stood, trying to get his bearings, and with a groan realised he didn't even know how to get back to the shed.

"Hell's bells," he said aloud, just as a large hand descended on his shoulder.

"Well, matey, what're you doing wandering about alone?" a gruff voice asked and the hand tightened its hold.

Ben looked up and into a pair of keen grey eyes set in a bearded face.

"Well?" the man asked again and Ben knew he was not going to let go until he got an answer.

"I'm lost." Ben's mind was working very fast. "I'm here on a scouts' trip and I got separated from the others."

As lies went, and though he didn't really like telling them, Ben thought this a good one. It seemed to be working too; the man had taken his hand off his shoulder.

"The leader will be mad," Ben went on. "They were heading for the dockers' canteen. Can you tell me where that is, please?" Knowing how grown-ups liked politeness he decided to lay it on a bit. "I'd be very grateful," he added. The man looked at him a little oddly.

"They're supposed to keep a tight rein on you lot when you come visiting here," he said, lifting his arm and pointing back the way Ben had come. "The canteen's that way. It's a grey building with a red..."

"Door." Ben finished for him, much relieved. "Thanks, I'd better hurry."

Without giving the man a chance to ask any more questions he started off at a brisk trot.

"Hey," the man called, "how come you scouts are doing a trip during the holidays?"

Ben kept going, pretending he hadn't heard. When the man called more loudly he broke into a run. One good sprint and he was outside the red door of the canteen.

He could hardly believe his luck! A *real* group of visiting children were lining up to get in. He could tell they were members of a club by the badges they wore.

No one noticed when he slipped into the canteen with them or noticed him queuing for drinks and sandwiches with them either.

There was no sign of Murt anywhere. To Ben's right was a room with some men playing snooker while straight in front of him stretched the canteen with its rows of long tables and red plastic chairs. None of the men sitting there, busily eating, was Murt. He was sure of that. None of them looked ugly enough. None of them seemed to be waiting for anyone, either. They all looked as if food was the only thing on their minds.

"Get a move on, son," said a voice behind him and Ben realised he was holding up the queue.

When he got to the thin, tired-looking woman behind the counter he asked for three cartons of milk and three sandwiches. Stuffing them in his pockets he sat at a table at the edge of the group, not too close in case any of the children decided to speak to him. As he started to eat his own sandwich he spotted Murt.

He was standing at one of the snooker tables, a cue in his hand and an ugly expression on his face. Daylight didn't improve his appearance one bit. His beady eyes darted to the door each time it opened. Everything about him seemed impatient and bad-tempered.

Ben took a gulp of his milk.

The canteen door opened and a man wearing a dark suit came in. Even though his glance around the canteen was casual, Ben somehow knew that this was Murt's accomplice. He even felt a wild urge to point Murt out to him—but of course he didn't. The man spotted Murt soon enough himself anyway and, after a curt nod, sat himself at another table. Murt, a scowl on his face, joined him.

"You're late," Ben could see Murt's lips forming the words but couldn't hear a thing. He would have to get closer. Murt lit a cigarette. He offered one to the other man but he refused, nodding to the walls where a sign said no smoking. Murt shrugged, blew some smoke in the air, then bent over the table, talking quickly. Ben watched the two men intently, trying to read their lips. He noticed that the second man had pale, cold eyes but he couldn't make out a word either of them was saying. He noticed too that they both stopped talking as soon as anyone came near.

Then it came to him, like a sudden flash lighting up his brain. The old spying trick. The one he and Bobby had used to eavesdrop on grown-ups years ago. When they were about six or seven. It would mean risking the loss of 20p or so but that was a chance he'd have to take.

Carefully, and without looking down, he slipped two coins out of his pocket. Making sure that no one saw him he dropped them, one by one, on to the floor so that they rolled in the direction of Murt's table. As soon as they were moving he stood up.

"Oops," he said, loudly and to no one in particular, "must have a hole in my pocket." Then he got down on his hands and knees and began to crawl in the direction of Murt's feet.

Murt was wearing brown boots. Ben felt very nervous

as he came close to them. He saw a pair of shiny black shoes opposite, just the kind to wear with a dark suit. He found one 10p near the black shoes and, making a pretence of looking for the other coin, managed to hear the most important part of the smugglers' conversation.

"We have to get those bags out of the shed before anyone starts asking questions," the owner of the shiny shoes was saying. His voice was as grey and cold as his eyes.

"We should move them tonight," Murt growled. "It's too risky leaving them and there'll be too many people about in the morning."

"Then you'll have to get here *very* early. Before anyone else…"

"What's wrong with tonight?" Murt sounded surlier than ever. "I'm here now. I can hang around for a few hours, nip in and get the stuff out of there in a flash. No one'll see me…"

"That's where you're wrong," the other voice was like a rapier. "The harbour police and their dogs are all over the place at night. You'd be nabbed within three minutes of getting to the shed. The early morning, just before the dockers get here, is the only time to do it."

"Look." Murt was getting angry. "I know my way around here. I know what to do…"

"You'll do as you're told." The other man's voice cut Murt off sharply. The amazing thing was that he hadn't even raised it. Murt, when next he spoke, was more subdued.

"All right, all right," he said, "no need to get heavy about it. I'll move in at seven bells and have the bags out of there in half an hour. No sweat."

"Good. That's more like it. You do what you're told and things will be all right. Just remember that and you'll be a happy and a rich man." Shiny shoes didn't sound very happy himself and when Murt answered, he sounded quite unhappy.

"You're sure there'll be a truck waiting?" he asked.

"The truck'll be there. Just you get those bags onto the quayside and leave the rest to me. Now you'd better get out of here."

"Mind if I finish my fag first?"

"Please yourself." The shiny shoes moved as their owner stood up, "but I'd advise you not to hang around too long. You're not exactly inconspicuous, are you, Murt?"

"What do you mean by that?"

"I mean people notice you. Not a good thing in your line of business." The man's soft laugh made Ben shiver. "Now get going and," he lowered his voice even more, "be sure to get back to the shed before seven in the morning."

Then he was gone, walking smartly across the floor. Ben waited until the door banged behind him before making a move. Just as he did, a lighting cigarette butt dropped beside him and one of Murt's boots ground it viciously into the ground. Backing away Ben spotted the second 10p, close to Murt's other boot.

Ben knew he should leave it there. But he reached for it anyway. It was a mistake. At that very moment Murt stood up, took a step and brought a boot right down on Ben's hand. Ben yelled, a cry of pure pain, and scrambled to his feet. As he raised his head he was close enough to feel Murt's hot breath on his face.

"What're you doing there?" Murt reached to grab him but Ben, having made one mistake, was not about to make another. Quick as a fox he made for the centre of the club group, now queuing to leave the canteen. As they pushed their way toward the door Ben kept his head down, willing them to move more quickly, all the while feeling Murt's eyes searching for him.

When they reached the door he looked up in relief— and straight into another adult face. A puzzled one this time.

"You're not one of our boys," said their owner but Ben, aware that delay would be fatal, didn't even wait to invent an answer. He made a dive through the door and began to run faster than he had ever run, in the direction of the transit shed.

9

The Biggest Spider in the World

While Ben was successfully completing his spying mission things were far from quiet in the transit shed. Not long after he left, Zaby, yawning, woke up.

"Do you want one of my blankets?" she asked Bobby. "You could have a sleep, too. It's safe up here. On the ground all sorts of things can get to you and bite you..."

"Maybe they can in Africa but not here," said Bobby, who didn't want to admit that he was afraid to sleep *anywhere* in the shed—floor, roof or even hanging out of the walls, until he knew what had frightened Murt.

"Not just in Africa," said Zaby in her practical way. "Don't you have mice here? And rats? And cockroaches?"

"Mice and rats. Yes, we have those all right. I'm not sure about cockroaches," said Bobby doubtfully. "What're they like?"

"Oh, they're black and shiny and they're about this size." Zaby demonstrated a size with two fingers. It seemed huge to Bobby.

"Are they like beetles?" he asked.

"Bigger. And they smell sometimes and they eat everything." Zaby yawned again. "I need some more sleep. Please don't talk to me any more."

Bobby would have liked to remind her that she was the one who had started the conversation but Zaby was asleep before he could say anything. He sighed. It wasn't very considerate of her to curl up in her blankets and leave him alone to imagine cockroaches and mice and rats all over the place. He hoped Ben had got to the canteen all right.

It was eerily silent in the shed and full of dark shadows. Bobby wished he could go outside where he could see through the gap in the door that the sun was still shining. He wasn't sure why he was so afraid. He called Zaby's name, softly, and just to see if she was sound asleep. "Zaby." He made it no more than a whisper. She didn't answer and he sighed. Lucky her. He wouldn't have minded a snooze himself but he knew there was no point in trying. The only place he felt like sleeping was in his own bunk with his football posters on the wall beside him. He hoped nothing would happen to them while he was away. He hoped his mother wouldn't tidy away the game he'd been playing before they left.

Out of nowhere a flood of terrible loneliness came over him. He just wanted to be at home, in his bedroom playing in the sun with his action men. He didn't care if the baby cried all day and all night. Or if his Mom and Dad ignored him all the time either. He just wanted to be where they were, among familiar things.

But it was too late now. He knew that. They had to keep going and get to Liverpool and Uncle John somehow. He couldn't let Ben down and he certainly couldn't chicken out in front of Zaby. What a laugh *she* would have if he did. A soft snore from her direction made him sigh again. He hated the darkness in here. He looked toward the door and the lure of the sun outside became impossible to resist.

Bobby left the cab, went to the door and pulled it open a little more. It made the usual grating sound but there seemed to be no one around to hear. The quayside was empty, with not a person in sight. He looked at the huge boat, almost empty of its cargo of cacao beans and Guinness modules. It seemed to be empty even of sailors.

At the thought of sailors, Bobby had a vision of Murt and looked nervously about. For all he knew, Murt might be back any minute for the bags. He might even have caught Ben and tortured him and found out about himself and Zaby! Better by far to be in the shed if he *did* come back. In there at least he could hide.

All the same, he left the door open when he went back into the shed. No point in closing off a way of escape. Zaby was still gently snoring. With no one to talk to he sat on the bags and studied the enormous bulk of the ship outside. As soon as she awoke he could ask Zaby exactly how they could get to the empty cabin. He was still convinced the *River Sokoto* was the ship for them, that they could...

Out of the corner of his eye Bobby saw a movement between the two bags beside him. His heart jumped, then began to beat a little faster than usual. Trying to keep calm he turned his head, slowly, and looked at the spot where he'd seen the movement. Nothing. There was nothing there. Just a dark hollow between two sacks. Nothing, nothing at all.

He was still telling himself there was nothing when he

saw the first long, hairy thing come poking out from between the bags. It was quickly followed by another, longer and even hairier. He could see the hairs quite clearly, even in the gloom of the shed. They were dark brown and they covered each one of the long, wavy things, more of which were emerging from between the bags. Bobby couldn't move, even though he knew that the things, tentacles or legs or whatever they were, must belong to some creature which would, any second now, pull its body out from between the bags.

Five of them had emerged when, sure enough, a body began slowly to appear. It was a truly horrible body, hairy and with sharp-looking fangs. It belonged to what Bobby reckoned must be the biggest spider in the world. As he found his voice and called hoarsely to Zaby, three more legs appeared.

There was no answer from Zaby and Bobby sat, too paralysed by fear to move. The spider—which was as big as a man's fist—stood looking poisonously at him.

Everything happened quickly then. Just as Bobby thought his end had come he heard Zaby's voice telling him calmly not to move.

"It won't harm you," she said, "if you stay still and don't frighten it."

Bobby didn't hear her leave the cab but, quite suddenly and silently, one of her blankets came through the air and landed over the spider and the bags. Next thing Zaby was grabbing his arm and pulling him off the bags and back into the fork-lift with her. For what seemed like hours he sat on the floor of the cab with his eyes tightly shut. When he opened them Zaby was rubbing his hands and looking very kindly at him.

"It's all right," she said, "everyone gets a fright like that the first time they see a tarantula."

"A tarantula!" Bobby gulped, staring at her. "That was a *tarantula*! They're *killers*! That must have been what frightened Murt! Unless..." an awful thought came to him, "there are more. Maybe he's not the only one. Maybe there are a whole lot of them..." He looked nervously around the cab.

"I don't think so," Zaby sounded reassuring. "It's strange enough for *one* to make the journey here. It has to be very warm for them to survive."

"So." Bobby had begun to shiver a bit, now that the first shock was over. "That could be Dublin's very first tarantula! And I've seen it! Wait'll I tell..." But to tell anyone he would have to get down from the fork-lift. He was never, ever going to get down from the fork-lift.

"Are there lots of tarantulas in Nigeria?" he asked, hoping Zaby wouldn't notice he was still frightened.

"Oh yes." Zaby was matter-of-fact. "They're the biggest of all spiders you know. Some of them live to be fifteen years old and are big enough to eat lizards and even frogs. But they eat cockroaches and beetles too. Anything they can lay their fangs on..."

"People too?" Bobby really wanted an answer to this.

"Of course they don't eat people. People are too big. They can poison people, sometimes. You might not die though, if a tarantula bit you. Other spiders are worse for killing. But the hairs are dangerous. They can make people get very sick."

Bobby himself was feeling pretty sick by now. "He was very big," he said weakly.

"He *is* one of the biggest I've ever seen," Zaby admitted,

"but he'll probably find himself a lizard and leave us alone."

"There are no lizards in Dublin," said Bobby miserably. Zaby tut-tutted.

"What sort of place *is* this?" she asked. "No cockroaches, no lizards! I hope at least you have some rats and mice for him to eat or it'll be the worse for us..."

"We have," said Bobby eagerly. "We've plenty of rats and mice. They'll keep him busy." He was mortified to see Zaby grinning widely. She knew he was still afraid. Then she decided to be kind again.

"I don't think he'll live very long here anyway. It's too cold and tarantulas are not really interested in people," she said, "so why don't we have a little sleep until Ben gets back?"

When she pulled the remaining blanket over them Bobby made no protest. It was warm underneath it, comfortable too when he curled up beside Zaby. In no time they were both asleep, snoring together in gentle harmony.

10

Sleeping with a Tarantula

It took Ben a while to get back to the shed. When he began running he was sure he was headed in the right direction but, after a few minutes, he realised he was lost in a maze of warehouses. He stopped then, forcing himself to think. To his relief, and once he looked around, he found he was able to take his bearings from the clearly visible funnel of the *River Sokoto*.

He was puffing and panting from the run by the time he slipped through the door of the shed. In the gloom everything was a dark blur but slowly his eyes readjusted and he saw the blanket covering the bags. He looked around for Bobby and Zaby. They were nowhere to be seen. "Bobby!" he called, as loudly as he dared. "Zaby— where are you? It's me. It's Ben."

There was no answer. He looked at the blanket in annoyance.

"What a dead giveaway," he muttered. "Anybody coming in could see that blanket." And he reached out a hand to pick it up.

"Ben, don't! Don't touch that blanket!"

Bobby's cry came just in time. Ben's fingers were within centimetres of grabbing the blanket.

"Leave it where it is! There's a poisonous tarantula underneath."

Ben jumped back as if the spider had already lunged at him.

"A *what*?" His voice came out as a loud squeak. Already nervous after his brush with Murt he was in no mood for new dangers just yet. Nor for jokes.

Bobby, summoning all his courage, climbed down from the cab and stood close to the fork-lift. He couldn't bring himself to cross to where Ben was standing by the bags.

"Are you trying to be funny?" he demanded, giving his younger brother a suspicious look.

"No." Bobby was indignant. "It nearly killed me. I was sitting there and it came right out from between the bags." He pointed. "It was just ready to attack me when Zaby threw that blanket over it. You should have seen it, Ben. It's *gigantic*! It's all hairy and has black fangs…"

"Better *not* to see it," said Zaby. "The next person who does might not be so lucky."

She had left the cab too and was sitting on one of the forks of the fork-lift. She looked across at Ben with a very serious face.

"So," she said to Ben, "what happened in the canteen?"

But Ben was still getting used to the idea that a real live tarantula was scuttling around the shed in which they were going to have to sleep. He didn't like the idea of spending the night under the same roof. Bobby, with a cautious look at the bags beside Ben, moved to sit next to Zaby on the forks. He felt a lot safer once he was off the ground. Ben felt very exposed, now the information about the tarantula had sunk in. He was, after all, standing where the spider might appear at any minute. Trying to appear casual he crossed to where the others sat on the forks. Wordlessly, they made room for him. Sitting close together all three of them studied the blanket for movement.

"He might have gone *into* a bag by now," Zaby said, "and have poisoned himself on cacao beans. Or he might be dead from cold…"

The boys thought either possibility quite likely. Certainly, the blanket was absolutely still. Either the tarantula wasn't there or it was dead.

"I brought you sandwiches and stuff," said Ben, remembering. He pulled the drinks and the by now pretty mushed sandwiches out of his pockets. He watched anxiously while a ravenous Bobby and Zaby began to eat.

"Don't drop any crumbs," he warned. "We don't want that monster climbing up here after food…"

"He won't," said Zaby confidently. "He likes to stay in dark corners."

"They're pretty horrible sandwiches anyway," said Bobby, finishing his and remembering what his mother was forever saying about hunger being good sauce. He'd never before known what she meant.

"Tell us what happened," he demanded of Ben, impatient now that his hunger was a little satisfied. "Did you see Murt? Did you hear his plans?"

"Of course I did." Ben frowned at the suggestion that he might have failed. "I heard everything."

Quickly, he told them all that he'd heard under the table and how he'd got away afterwards.

"Murt'll be here before seven in the morning," he concluded, "so we'd better put our heads together about what we're going to do…"

"…and we'll have to do it before he gets here," Bobby finished for him.

Ben furrowed his brow, and a variety of ideas flashed through his brain. They could place a trip wire across the door or booby trap it. Either way Murt could still pick himself up and get to the bags. They could jam the door shut but Murt was sure to force it open somehow. Zaby looked at the bags.

"I know," she said, "we can open the bags, empty out the beans, find the drugs and hide them."

She made it sound very easy. The boys would have liked to find fault with her idea, but the more they thought about it the better it sounded.

"But," Ben eventually spotted a flaw, "where will we hide the drugs?"

"I don't know," Zaby admitted, "you're the ones who say you know Dublin docks. Behind this shed somewhere, I suppose. We'll have to get out before Murt comes at seven o'clock, anyway. We can take them with us and hide them in another shed."

"Yes," said Bobby excitedly. "We can find a really safe place and when we get to Liverpool, Uncle John can ring up and tell the police here where they are! It's a brilliant idea…"

"Not bad at all," Ben conceded, feeling a little left out but recognising a good plan when he heard one. Zaby acknowledged the praise with a gracious nod of her head.

With so much happening they hadn't felt the time

passing. But it was almost nine o'clock now and beginning to get dark outside. The shadows in the shed had got darker, mysteriously creeping out of corners, round by the pile of cacao beans and up to the foot of the fork-lift. Bobby was the one who expressed what they were all thinking.

"Who's going to lift the blanket off?" he asked.

There was dead silence from the other two. The image of the lurking tarantula was real and horrible to everyone, even to Ben, who hadn't seen him. Bobby's description had been enough. All three of them wanted desperately to believe that the tarantula was starved, frozen and definitely dead. Only, somehow, the darker it got the larger he became in their imaginations. And the more dangerous. That was the thing Bobby hated about the dark. Everything, even things which didn't frighten you during the day, became scary.

"Why don't we go to sleep now," Bobby suggested. "We'll be awake long before seven o'clock and we can move the bags then."

"Good idea." Ben made his voice very strong in case Zaby should think he was chickening out. "It'll be much easier in the morning light." He was really tired, anyway. The result, he supposed, of not sleeping the night before.

11

An Enemy Captured

They had to squeeze together in the cab but at least they were warm and felt safe. Soon the last bit of light had left the sky outside and the shed had become inky black and spookier than ever. Bobby began making a funny sound and Ben realised he was trying to whistle. He was always trying to whistle—and never succeeding.

"Shut up, Bobby," he said. But Bobby kept on trying.

"I vote we give the tarantula a name," said Ben. "I think we should call him Dracula. Then this shed can be Dracula's Crypt."

"Well I vote against that," said Bobby and stopped whistling. A ghostly rustling came from one of the dark corners. He began to whistle again.

"I wonder," said Zaby, "what time it is at home. I wonder what they're doing..."

She turned away from the boys and pulled herself into a ball, arms hugging her knees. Her head was down and she didn't make a sound but the boys knew she was crying. They didn't dare to make any of the usual remarks about whinging girls. They didn't even want to because they knew exactly how she was feeling. They were feeling pretty lonely themselves and, now that the excitement of the day was over, more than a little worried. They'd been away from home less than a day. Zaby was away a whole week now and she'd been alone most of that time. Neither boy was at all sure he could have done what she'd done, alone. So they let her cry for a few minutes, embarrassed but sympathetic.

"I've got a piece of chocolate left," Ben said eventually, "do you want it?"

Zaby shook her head. Her whole body seemed to shake with it.

"Look," Ben went on kindly, "you could go home on the *River Sokoto*, you know. And the captain is sure to phone your parents."

Zaby said nothing. They could tell she'd stopped crying, though. They waited, tactfully, until she was able to talk without tears in her voice.

"I know," she said at last, "it's just that there will be such a row and they'll be angry with me all the way home. I know they will."

Ben had one of his flashes of inspiration. He whispered it to Bobby, then turned to Zaby, talking all in a rush.

"We've decided you can come to Liverpool with us. Uncle John will talk to the captain of the *River Sokoto* and sort things out..." Zaby lifted her head.

"Can I? Can I really come with you? I could find that empty cabin and we could all slip in there tomorrow evening and..."

They talked and planned for a long time after that. They talked until they became too tired to notice the strange night-time sounds in the shed and until its darkness became a soothing thing which lulled them to sleep.

They awoke to light streaming through the door and the sound of seagulls loud outside.

For a while Ben lay, lazily half-asleep, wondering exactly what was different about the morning. The sound of the gulls was quite usual, so was the hooting of boats in the distance. But his bunk had become small and hard and cramped...He opened his eyes and remembered everything. He looked at Bobby, also struggling to wake up, and guessed he must be feeling the same way. Zaby was still asleep.

Ben's watch said six o'clock. Not bad. They had an hour to empty the cacao beans and get out of the shed with the drugs. He gave Zaby a poke in the ribs and she woke, looking just as confused as he and Bobby had been. They left the fork-lift and stretched their cramped bodies on the floor of the shed.

"Might as well have some breakfast," said Bobby, holding out a sorry-looking apple, the very last of the fruit. They broke the remaining piece of chocolate in three and got two small bites each of the apple. It was better than nothing.

"First," said Ben, "we'll have to take the blanket off..."

No one said anything. No one wanted to be the one to touch it.

"We'll toss," suggested Bobby. Zaby shook her head.

"No," she said, "we must all do it together."

Which is what they did, each taking a corner and pulling, gently at first and then, on the count of three, with a quick tug which pulled the blanket clean away from the bags. The tarantula fell with a thud onto the ground in front of them and they jumped back. It immediately began to move groggily around in a circle.

"He's not dead," said Bobby, his voice a mixture of shock and dismay.

But, strangely, he was not so afraid of the tarantula any longer. For one thing, the spider looked pretty weak. For another, he now felt bigger, stronger and cleverer than any spider. Finally, because an idea had come to him.

Slowly, slowly, Bobby reached behind to where they'd left the empty lunch-box. Still slowly he took the lid off and then, lid in one hand and box in the other, began to inch toward the giant spider. Before the others could do anything to stop him he'd lunged forward and trapped the tarantula inside, pinning him to the floor. They could see him through the plastic, his legs furiously beating against the sides of the box.

Still working very, very slowly, Bobby slipped the lid underneath the box. A leg began to snake its way out of the box and Zaby and Ben caught their breaths in horrified gasps. But Bobby pressed down on the box and the leg retreated inside again. He immediately snapped box and lid together and the tarantula was a prisoner.

"Public enemy number one safely captured," Bobby said, standing up and waving the box triumphantly. Zaby clapped her hands in delight and, to Bobby's absolute mortification, put an arm around him and gave him a kiss. He could feel his face burning and was glad for just that moment that they weren't outside in the sunlight.

"Lay off," he said, shaking himself free and putting down the box.

Ben picked it up and began punching holes with his Don't Bug Me badge.

"Might as well allow old Dracula to breathe," he said. "Maybe we can bring him to the Zoo or something."

They put the lunch-box in the schoolbag and faced the job of emptying the cacao bags. It was harder than they'd thought to open them but at last they managed to open one and tip it over. The beans spilled across the floor like a dark brown sea and Ben felt a wild urge to dive into the middle of them.

They had started to open a second bag when the light from the doorway was cut off and a heavy shadow darkened everything.

"What the hell do you kids think you're doing?" Murt's voice was a vicious hiss as he came hulking across the shed toward them.

12

An Enemy Gives Chase

As Murt advanced on the children, swinging his arms, he seemed terrifyingly like a gorilla. None of them said anything or moved an inch. Their mouths had dried up and they couldn't seem to find their voices. Their feet had become stuck to the ground. Murt kept on coming and it was as if he was spreading himself all across the shed.

"What're you doing with them bags?" he snarled as he got closer. "Answer me, you brats."

They could see how mad his eyes were and sense the crazy anger in him. Still no one answered. It wasn't so much that their frozen larynx couldn't get the words out. It was just that they knew, somehow, that no matter what they said Murt wouldn't hear. He didn't want to listen. He wanted to do them harm.

"Run!" Ben was the first to find his voice and its sound broke the spell of paralysing fear which had gripped them.

As Murt took another lumbering step they began to run toward the fork-lift. Murt, who had expected them to head for the door, was momentarily thrown off guard and stopped. This gave the children just enough time to begin climbing into the cab of the fork-lift. They had pulled the door closed before Murt, with a howl, started after them. By the time he reached the fork-lift, they had locked the cab door.

"Get down from there." Murt's voice rumbled like thunder. "Get down! If I have to come after you you'll be sorry, *very* sorry!"

"No way." Ben's voice sounded braver than he felt and gave courage to Bobby and Zaby. They felt reasonably safe in the cab too, which now seemed to them almost like an old friend. Murt, his face red, shook his fist at them. Zaby stuck out her tongue and Bobby picked up a wrench and shook it at him.

They knew immediately that these actions were not a good idea. Murt became so angry he seemed in danger of blowing up in front of their eyes. Then, with a King Kong-like roar, he charged at the fork-lift. The whole vehicle shook with the weight of his body as he grappled with the door handle. Too late the children realised the lock was not at all strong. They held the handle on their side but Murt was stronger and the door slowly began to open. As Murt's stubby, powerful fingers came around the door, Ben, with all his strength, brought the wrench down across the knuckles.

The door swung open and, with a blood-curdling yell and a stream of curses, Murt jumped back holding his hand.

"Out of the way, out of the way." Zaby's voice was full of urgency. The boys moved just in time to allow her second blanket to sail past and drop right over Murt.

While he floundered, his bellows smothered beneath the blanket, Zaby and the boys clambered from the fork-lift and made their escape from the shed.

But not before Bobby had grabbed his schoolbag with the lunch-box and Dracula inside, which was strange because Bobby was one of those children who never remembered his lunch-box when he was *supposed* to.

Afterwards, no one believed him when he explained why he'd remembered it as they rushed from the cab. He had, he said, heard his mother's voice. Clear as a bell she'd called, "Bobby, for goodness sake pick up your lunch-box." So he did. And was very glad later in the day that he had...

They ran until they reached the cover of a stack of timber. From there Ben sneaked a look and saw Murt stagger to the shed doorway, disentangling himself from the blanket. As Ben watched, he viciously kicked the blanket away from him and began to make in their direction.

"Let's go," Ben said urgently.

Dodging from timber stack to timber stack they made their way toward what they hoped were the gates of the docks. No sound came from behind them and they began to slow down, to feel safe at last.

Without warning, Murt appeared in front of them. They had forgotten that he would know his way around the docks, that, having seen the direction they took, he would have figured out a way to head them off. He was so close now they could see the perspiration on his face. They stopped. They had come to the end of the stacked timber. Their only hope now lay in making a sideways run for the nearest road heading for the docks entrance. Desperately, Bobby held up the lunch-box, shook it in Murt's face. As the smuggler took a frantic step backward the three of them took deep breaths and sprinted. Behind them they could hear the harsh, strangled sounds of Murt's breathing.

They had almost reached the turning for the road when Zaby slipped. "Yeow!" she cried and rolled over, holding her knee. The boys stopped, did a sort of wheeling turn, grabbed one of Zaby's arms each and pulled her to her feet. Blood streamed down her leg and there was a dazed expression on her face.

"Try to run," Ben commanded as they pulled her along with them. Soon, biting her lip because of the pain, Zaby was running as fast as the boys. But the delay had allowed Murt to gain ground and they could hear him panting noisily as he caught up. They kept on running, not bothering to look for cover, just hoping they could outrun him.

They came to a sort of crossroads and a sign which read City Centre. With a new burst of energy they followed the sign until they came to a wide road which was criss-crossed with railway tracks. A goods train, with two men walking carefully just in front of it, was making its very slow way along the tracks. As the children came flying on to the road one of the men saw them.

"Hey, watch it," he cried. "Are you trying to get us all killed?"

But the children raced on across the tracks until they reached cover on the other side of the train. They could see words like Acrylonitrile and Danger written all over it but still they didn't stop, just kept heading for the gates of the docks. The road ahead was wide and empty but, at the end, they could see the security box occupied by the harbour police.

When they looked back, they could see Murt's legs coming up fast on the other side of the train. They knew the two men must be guarding something terribly explosive on the train and couldn't help them. They reached the head of the train and one of the men, who was using a walkie-talkie, made furious signals to them.

"Get away," he cried. "Get away from here. It's dangerous..."

Murt's pounding feet sounded frighteningly close. This was not, Ben realised, the place to face him. Murt was capable of anything, even of blowing up the train.

"Look!" It was Bobby who spotted the dry-dock and the hiding place promised by the tired-looking ship resting there for repairs. If they could manage to hide for a while, the harbour police were bound to arrive and put an end to the chase. As they veered left and into a frantic run toward the dry-dock the train went slowly on toward the gates.

They were almost there when behind them the wheezing sounds of Murt stopped. Looking back, Ben saw a car coming to a stop alongside Murt and a familiar man in a dark suit getting out.

"Faster," Ben cried. "The other one's here..."

They came to the edge of the dry-dock. The hull and propeller of the ship being repaired seemed an awfully long way down.

"How're we supposed to get down there?" Zaby's leg

was still bleeding and the boys could tell she wanted to rest.

As the three of them looked into the well of the dry-dock they could hear the sound of running feet.

"Come on!" said Bobby. "We'll have to get down there before they see us!"

They lowered themselves, one by one, and as far as they could, before letting go to drop on to the concrete floor of the dry-dock. When they reached the cover of the ship's propeller they stopped. Crouched tightly together, they could hear Murt and his companion stop in confusion above them.

"They can't have got very far," said Murt.

"They'd better not." His companion's voice was pure steel. "Because you, matey, as well as those brats, will be for the chop if this operation gets blown!"

13

An Enemy with a Gun

In the still, bright silence of the morning, everything the men said drifted down to the children, clear and clipped like the air. All of it was nasty and threatening.

"It's getting late." Murt's companion began to pace up and down. Ben could see his shiny shoes again. "You'd better get back to that transit shed. Get the stuff out of there before the dockers come on at eight o'clock. Quick, man, move."

"But what about the kids? We can't just leave them wandering about. They'll..."

"*I'll* worry about the kids. I'll keep them here." The other voice cut sharply through Murt's low growl. "You just get the hell out of here and back to the shed. If anything happens to that consignment it'll be your head on the block, remember that!"

Without a word, Murt began to run, though not back the way they had come. He probably knew another short-cut.

"The harbour police will be looking for us, and for Murt, by now," Bobby whispered. "The men on the train will have told them. They'll catch Murt..."

"Maybe not," whispered Ben. "He knows how to keep out of sight around here. And they don't know about the bags in the transit shed…"

In fierce whispers they discussed the situation. There was, they realised, a good chance that Murt would get the bags, and the drugs in them, free of the docks before the harbour police realised exactly what was going on. Because the man with the gun was blocking the way they weren't going to be able to get to the harbour police HQ at the docks' entrance. One or all of them would have to get back to the transit shed and raise the alarm from there.

They could see the other man clearly now. He had come to the edge of the dry-dock and was leaning over, scanning the area with his pale eyes, missing nothing. The expression on his face was not the sort which made you feel good. His face was in some ways more frightening than Murt's swollen, angry face had been.

As they watched he pulled a gun from his pocket and called down to them. His voice, low and hard, was far more sinister than Murt's bluster.

"If you lot so much as breathe loudly, I'll blow your silly little heads off." Then they saw that he was smiling. "I don't like children. They should be seen and not heard. They're selfish, troublesome creatures and they get in the way. You three have got in the way of very important adult business…"

As he spoke he walked slowly along the top of the dock, his eyes fixed all the time on the hull of the ship.

"He can't see us," Ben whispered. "He doesn't know where we are but he's hoping we'll give ourselves away if he keeps talking long enough…"

"You're right," whispered Zaby, "but even so I believe him. I think he really would blow our heads off…"

"*If* he sees us," said Bobby. "We must keep out of sight…"

"Look." Ben had been thinking. "If Murt gets the drugs out of the docks the man with the gun is going to come down here after us. We've seen them, we can tell the police what they look like. We *have* to get out of here and back to the shed."

A chill crept over the others as they realised Ben was right. The man was standing above them now, looking at his watch. Every minute which passed brought Murt closer to the transit shed and the men's plan closer to success.

Ben was looking around him. Then he had an idea, one of those flashes of brilliance which sometimes came to him at just the right times. Two things put it into his head. The first was the wide plank of timber lying at their feet. He picked it up. It was, as he'd thought, just about his own height.

"Keep still," Bobby hissed.

Ben ignored him. As slowly as he could he slipped off his jacket and, very carefully, hung it over the plank. Bobby and Zaby saw then what he was planning. From where the man stood, and if he was allowed see only a part of it, the plank would look like the back of a boy.

Bobby looked doubtful. "It won't work," he whispered.

"It will. Anyway, have you a better plan?"

Not waiting for an answer Ben began to inch the jacket-wrapped plank forward. As he did so Zaby, whose leg had stopped bleeding, looked around and spotted the other thing which had given Ben the idea.

"It *will* work," she whispered to Bobby and pointed, "if we use that ladder while the man's attention is on the jacket."

The ladder, a metal one, was attached to the wall at the other end of the dry-dock.

"That's it," said Ben. "That's my plan. Now, as soon as he spots the jacket, we start moving. Right?"

The others nodded nervously as he gave the plank a final nudge into the man's view.

"Hold it, hold it right there." His voice came down to them, sharp as a pistol shot. "One more move and I'll shoot.   Just stay as you are for another five minutes. If you do that, I might even be persuaded to let you go…"

While he was talking, Bobby, Ben and Zaby made their quick, stealthy way to the ladder. Hidden from the man's view by the ship they clambered up and found themselves beside a set of pipelines. Beyond them was a crane.

Keeping low they nipped between the pipelines, around the crane and on to a clear stretch of quayside. Silently Ben pointed and silently they started in the direction of the distant funnel of the *River Sokoto*.

14

Spilling the Cacao Beans

The run back to the ship didn't take long. With caution thrown to the winds in the children's desire to foil Murt's plan, the journey seemed to take only minutes.

The quayside was full of activity when they got there. Dockers had begun unloading the rest of the cargo, a second crane had moved in and the sailors were busy with jobs of their own. No one noticed the children, hiding by the side of the transit shed. Of Murt there was no sign.

"We could just go over and tell them everything," said Ben, though without conviction.

"No, we couldn't." Bobby was adamant. "They'd never believe us. And by the time we'd explained and everything was sorted out, Murt would be clear away from the docks with the drugs."

"And I'd be back on the *River Sokoto*." Zaby sounded quite desolate.

"It was just an idea," said Ben hurriedly, wishing he'd kept his mouth shut. "Look! There he is."

Murt was coming out of the shed, driving the fork-lift. It was piled high with the cacao bags and he looked, to everyone but the children, to be just another worker. The dockers obviously thought so anyway because no one paid the slightest attention to him as he expertly turned the fork-lift and headed toward a small, red truck at the other end of the quayside.

"We can't let him get away with it," said Ben, fiercely.

"No, we can't," said Bobby, equally fierce.

They looked at one another, a look that said "here goes." Both knew there was nothing for it but to break from the cover of the shed and go after Murt themselves.

"You stay here," Ben said to Zaby, using his bossiest tone to make sure she would do as he said, "and don't move until we come back."

The truth was that he'd no idea how they were going to get back. Once they revealed themselves on the quayside there was no knowing what would happen. He just thought it best for her to stay out of the way.

"Here, Zaby." Bobby took the schoolbag off his back, "you look after Dracula. He's the only tarantula in Dublin so don't lose him…"

Then the boys were gone, after Murt and the slow-moving fork-lift, running as fast as their tired legs would carry them. Ignoring shouts from the dockers, they ran until they caught up with their quarry.

Murt, intent on guiding the fork-lift, didn't see them until their two pairs of hands laid hold of a bag from among the pile on his fork-lift. His face took on a look of complete disbelief and became quite purple as he tried to turn the fork-lift. But the boys were not about to let go now, not when they had come so far in their attempts to foil the drug-smuggling plot. With all their strength they pulled at the bag. It seemed immovable until Murt, unwittingly, helped them.

Intent on stopping them, he put the fork-lift into reverse. The sudden change in direction, along with the boys tugging, unsettled the bag completely and it toppled over, crashing to the ground at their feet. Worse, from Murt's point of view, was that it unsettled a second bag, which fell with an even greater crash, on to the hard concrete of the quayside.

Murt attempted to change direction again, roaring at them from the cab. He seemed to be trying to run over Ben and Bobby as he put the vehicle into forward motion with a ferocious scrunching of gears.

But the fork-lift didn't run over the boys. Instead, with a crackle that sounded sickeningly like the sound of ten thousand beetles being squashed, it ran over the two fallen bags. The cacao beans, millions and millions of them, tumbled out and all over the concrete, sending their delicious chocolaty smell Ben and Bobby's way.

But something else came out of the bags too. Something white and powdery, which had been hidden in the heart of the cacao beans, wrapped in clear plastic bags.

"The drugs," breathed Bobby. "That must be the drugs."

15

A Spider to the Rescue

A stunned silence descended on the quayside while everyone took in what had happened. The dockers stopped work and the sailors gathered in a quiet, watchful group. Murt had stopped the fork-lift, frozen by the realisation that the game was up.

Everything happened quickly then. As two of the dockers began to run toward them, the boys heard the cab door opening. Instinctively, hoping to hold Murt until the dockers reached them, they pushed with all their might against the door.

"We'll never do it!" Ben shouted as Murt heaved against the door. "Jump back!"

They moved just as Murt came crashing out of the cab.

"I'll get you brats," he yelled. "I'll get you if it's the last thing I do."

Then he was off, running fast and with the dockers in pursuit. In the distance the whine of a police siren had started up and Murt stopped, looking frantically around for another way of escape. What he found instead was a long, heavy-looking metal bar which he picked up and began to whirl in the air above his head.

"Keep back!" he yelled.

The dockers stopped, then jumped out of the way as Murt turned, swinging the bar, ran back the way he had come and disappeared around the end of the shed. Two police cars came speeding along the quay and, after them, a couple of German shepherd dogs pulling their policemen handlers.

"He's making for the oil jetties," cried a docker from the other end of the quay. "That's the most dangerous part of the docks! We could all be blown sky-high if someone doesn't stop him! If he damages or knocks against a pipe the whole place could go up!"

In the commotion everyone had forgotten about the boys—and the boys had forgotten about Zaby. They were just about to join in the chase when her voice came in a loud whisper behind them.

"What about me?" it demanded. "Are you going to leave me here?"

Looking around they saw her brown arm signal from behind the door of the transit shed.

"I thought we told you to stay by the side of the shed?" Ben hissed furiously.

"And I thought it would be better to hide in here," Zaby said.

"Anyway, no point in hiding any more. Too many people have seen us by now. Come on..."

Zaby came out of the shed, Bobby's schoolbag on her back. She hugged herself as she came toward them.

"I'm cold," she complained.

"Get a move on." Bobby couldn't wait to join the

chase. "Let's see what's happening..."

It was strange to be running openly, past the *River Sokoto* and the amazed stares of the Nigerian sailors. Ahead, the police sirens had stopped and things had become strangely quiet. As they came round the other end of the shed they discovered why.

In front of them was an oil jetty. There was no mistaking it. A tanker was berthed alongside and oil pipelines, like rows of fat, black snakes, joined the two. Signs everywhere warned of danger.

But the jetty was packed with people now. The harbour police had got out of their cars and taken up silent positions along its length. The dockers stood behind them, silent and alert. Even the dogs had become quiet, standing with their handlers. Beyond them all, balanced on the pipelines and with a wild expression on his face, stood Murt. He was holding the metal bar above his head. As the children watched, a harbour policeman reached inside his car. Murt saw him.

"One more move and you're all dead," his voice was very loud in the strange silence. "Anyone else moves and I'll smash this pipeline, blow us all to kingdom come. Keep back."

"He's nuts," a docker close to the children said. "He'll do it too. Best not to go near him."

"If he smashes that pipeline," said another, "he won't just blow us up. The whole port and docks will go too..."

The policeman, very slowly, took out a large megaphone and raised it in front of his face. "You can't escape," he called. "We have your accomplice in custody. It's all over. You might as well give yourself up."

Murt's answer was to shake the iron bar in the air, almost losing his balance in the process. It seemed, for a fearful moment, that he might fall and accidentally blow them all up anyway. But he regained his balance, and his voice.

"Let no one come near me," he called again. "Let no one move." No one did. It was obvious that Murt was in a very nervous state and likely to do anything.

"It's our fault," said Ben softly. "We let him get away. We have to do something."

"I think I know what we can do," said Zaby, equally softly. "I've thought of a plan. Listen."

The boys listened. It was a daring and risky plan. There was a chance it might not work. But there was a much greater chance of Murt blowing up everyone and everything in the docks in the next five minutes if someone didn't do something. Since they possessed the means of paralysing Murt, it was up to the children to do that something.

"Right." Zaby was businesslike. "You two go and make a fuss. Let the police and Murt and everyone see you. I'll start moving in with Dracula."

"I don't see why you have to be the one to do it." Ben looked worried.

But Zaby, the lunch-box firmly held under her arm, had started to make her stealthy way toward the pipelines.

"Good luck," Ben called after her.

"Good luck," Bobby echoed. Zaby gave a small wave and a grin and then the boys walked, very slowly so as not to startle Murt, from behind the container. He saw them almost immediately.

"I'll get you brats," he yelled. "I'll get you..."

At just the right time all eyes turned on the boys. Zaby, unseen, slipped between the pipelines and began to creep toward Murt.

"We've heard about you," a concerned policeman said to the boys. "Quick, get into the car." Reluctantly, the boys did so.

Zaby was only a few feet away from Murt. He was still yelling that he would get the boys, even if it was the last thing he did. "Probably *will* be, if this plan doesn't work," Zaby thought grimly. When she was close enough to touch Murt's foot she began, working so slowly her fingers ached, to open the lunch-box. As soon as he felt air the tarantula began to move, out of the lunch-box and on to the pipeline. He stood, hairy and terrifying as ever, right in front of Murt.

Murt was the last to see him. Zaby had by now been spotted from the quayside and all eyes were fixed on the tarantula as it began to make its way toward Murt's foot. He stopped shouting at last and, following the gaze of the crowd, looked down and saw the spider.

Zaby, closest to him, saw the cold sweat break out on his face. He became absolutely rigid, the way he had before, and his eyes stared. The tarantula went on crawling, shaking itself a little as it went. But Murt could not have moved to save his life. When his nerveless fingers dropped the metal bar, Zaby deftly caught it. She could hear the deep breath of relief which came from the quayside.

Still Murt went on standing there, frozen with fear, unaware of anything but the approaching spider. He didn't even seem to notice when two policemen arrived and quietly led him off the pipeline. Dracula, annoyed by the bright light and seeing the prospect of cover disappear with Murt's boot, vanished forever beneath the pipelines.

16

A Holiday at Last

It was a week later and Zaby, Ben and Bobby were sitting on the beach at Sandymount. They were watching a boat as it came slowly out of the docks and moved out across the blue of the bay.

"I wonder if he's still alive," said Bobby.

"Could be," said Zaby, trailing her hand in a pool of water. She had got used to the climate and didn't think it half so cold now.

"He was a pretty strong spider," Bobby went on, "and pretty clever. Maybe he found a home under the pipelines. Somewhere filled with beetles and rats and things for him to eat. Maybe he's stuffing himself and growing bigger and bigger."

"Maybe," said Ben. "And maybe he'll come out some day when he's as big as a dog."

"Or a horse. Maybe he'll grow as big as a horse."

They had a bit of a laugh then, at the idea of a horse-sized tarantula. Then they played in the pool, poking around for sea-horses to show Zaby. They'd brought her to see the Liffey too, both in town and in the mountains. She'd been very impressed.

"How big do tarantulas grow?" Ben asked Zaby after a while.

"Dracula was one of the biggest I ever saw," Zaby answered. "I don't think they grow much bigger than him."

"My lunch-box is still back there," said Bobby. "It's probably still on the pipeline. Maybe we should go back and get it. We could look around for old Dracula while we were there."

"Mom's got you a new lunch-box," Ben said.

"I know," said Bobby and they all sighed because they knew the great adventure was really over and that there was no going back. You couldn't make things happen a second time. Not the same way anyhow. Zaby was due to go home the next day. When she went things would be *really* over.

After the police had arrested Murt things had happened quickly. The children had been whisked away in a car to harbour police headquarters. The boys' parents had been sent for and Zaby's had been telephoned. There had been a lot of talking and explaining to the police and other important, serious-looking people. Some of them had praised the children, others had been most annoyed. Murt, Shiny Shoes and the Nigerian sailor had all been arrested and the children hadn't seen them again.

Ben and Bobby's parents had been more relieved than annoyed. They had been terribly worried about the boys and had been to the police to report them missing. They had a zillion questions to ask but had been so glad to see Ben and Bobby that it had taken them two whole days to get round to telling them off about leaving home. When they did, the boys had had to agree with some of the things they said. Trying to stow away had, they knew, been a dangerous thing to do. And they should have said how they felt about Sinéad and talked to their parents about being left out and neglected. Their parents certainly listened now, very thoughtfully and quietly, when the boys explained about how they had been feeling all summer. Their mother even apologised when they'd finished.

"We are so sorry, boys," she'd said. "We just didn't think. We thought that you would understand a small baby needs lots of attention in the beginning—and that you would know we loved you as much as ever."

"Yes," said their Dad. "We should have discussed things with you. Especially about the playroom. We've been thinking, in fact, that the house is a bit small now. Maybe we should move…"

"Oh no!" the boys cried together.

"We don't want to move," Ben said. "That's why Zaby stowed away."

Zaby had not been sent back to Nigeria on the *River Sokoto*. She was, after all, a heroine. When she finished telling her story to two very concerned people from the Nigerian Embassy, it was decided she needed time to recuperate, and to have her knee looked at, before going home. After a phone call that seemed to go on forever, Zaby's parents, who had thought they would never see their daughter again, agreed to allow her to stay with the Kilroys for a week.

Then there had been the fuss made by the newspapers and television. Because they had exposed a notorious international drug-smuggling ring, the children had been quite famous, for a few days anyway. They were treated like celebrities by the photographers and reporters who came to take their pictures and ask them questions.

It was all great fun, better than any holiday could have been. Even so, they were careful not to take all the credit and told the reporters, and anyone else who would listen to them, that it was Dracula who, in the end, had been the real saviour of the docks. It was strange how, over the days which followed and at the most unlikely of times, his hairy image would surface to haunt the three children. They couldn't help wondering what had happened to him.

Zaby fitted in perfectly with the Kilroy family. Of course she was ten years old and not a baby but even so it filled the boys with hope for the future. Life with a sister might not be so bad after all. Certainly, if Sinéad grew up anything like Zaby she would be worth having around. (Zaby, they discovered, was good at all sorts of games and even showed them some pretty interesting new ones.)

There was so much to show Zaby, and so many things to do before she went home, that the week became a real holiday for everyone. Even Sinéad, who seemed to have got over her terrible crying habit, laughed and gurgled when Zaby played with her. Zaby liked Sinéad, but that was to be expected. Girls usually liked babies. What the boys hadn't expected, and what in fact happened pretty quickly, was that they grew to like Sinéad themselves.

Another change was that Ben seemed to have lost his appetite for chocolate—which wasn't surprising in the circumstances.

So, as they sat on the beach watching the ship, the boys tried not to think about tomorrow being Zaby's last day in Dublin. Zaby herself felt both excited and sad. She was looking forward to seeing her parents again and to the plane trip home. But she was sad to be leaving her friends—and the whole new world she'd discovered.

"That boat looks a bit like a giant whale," she said, squinting as it crossed the horizon and disappeared from view.

"It's probably going to Liverpool," said Bobby.

"Liverpool! Who cares about Liverpool!" said Ben. "I reckon, if we put our heads together, that we could figure out a way to get to Nigeria for our summer holidays next year."

"That would be great," Zaby cried. "Maybe we could ask for it as a reward for catching the smugglers!

Putting their heads together, they began to plan.

About Dublin's Port and Docks

Dublin, like most of the world's important cities, came about because of a river. Long ago, when invaders came to a country, they needed a place to tie up their boats—so they had to be able to go up a river.

In Dublin's case, the river was the Liffey and the invaders were the Danish Vikings who came here in their longboats in the ninth century AD. They sailed up the Liffey and set up a settlement in Wood Quay in about 841. For reasons we'll never know they didn't stay long—eighty years or so. But Dublin and its port have their origins in that first settlement.

The next settlement, on exactly the same spot, was founded by Norse invaders in the year 917. It survived, grew rich and strong, and over the years has become the Dublin we know today.

Those early Vikings established Dublin as an important port city. By the twelfth century there were 200 ships trading out of Dublin with England and Europe. As trading links grew across the world so did the city and port. During the eighteenth century, especially, the port facilities were greatly improved. The Grand Canal Docks were opened in 1796 and the Custom House Docks in the 1820s. The Dublin Port and Docks Board, the organisation that runs things today, took over in 1867. Over the years they have greatly developed the port, adding quays and reclaiming land.

Engineers and builders working for the Port and Docks Board would have built the quays across which

the boys and Zaby ran and against which the *River Sokoto*
was berthed. They were responsible too for the sheds,
warehouses, storage areas, roads and railway.

Facts About Today's Dublin Port and Docks

There are two dry-docks (or graving docks) in Dublin port. The first was built in 1860 and the second, the one in which the children hid, was opened in 1957. The oil zone covers 41 hectares. There is space too for the storage of acrylonitrile—the very dangerous and highly explosive substance being carried in the slow-moving train near the end of the story.

There are two oil jetties. The eastern oil jetty has twenty-one pipelines linking it to the oil zone and the western jetty has fifteen pipelines.

There are rail marshalling yards and tracks which link Dublin's docks with the rest of the country's railway system.

Pilots from the port pilot ships in through the narrower straits of Dublin Bay. Tugboats are sometimes used for the same reason.

There are about 55 members of the harbour police force. The force has fire-fighting and dog-handling units. German Shepherd dogs are used and they patrol mostly at night-time.

Ships from West Africa and Nigeria are frequent callers to Dublin Port. They bring mostly cacao beans, mahogany timber and Guinness beer modules.

Stowaways are often discovered on board too.

The method of carrying cargo on the *River Sokoto*, seen being unloaded by Ben and Bobby, is called break bulk. Very few ships still carry goods this way and break bulk is fast becoming a thing of the past. Nowadays almost all ships carry their cargo in containers. The boys and Zaby were lucky; it would not have been possible to get at the cacao beans and have their adventure if the *River Sokoto* had been carrying all her cargo in containers.

It is not impossible for a tarantula to arrive in Dublin docks. It would be impossible to stow away in the fashion planned by Ben and Bobby. The harbour police are a vigilant force.

The Boy Who Saved Christmas

By

Vincent McDonnell

Why should Christmas need to be saved? Because it is in real danger of being lost!

Not many people knew it: it was all hushed up, of course. Santa Claus was kidnapped by the vilest gang of crooks that ever lived. The bravery and intelligence of computerwise Timmy Goodfellow and his animal friends are sorely needed, otherwise Christmas might disappear—for ever!

Vincent McDonnell was the recipient of the GPA First Fiction award in 1989. This is his first book for children.

A Monster Called Charlie

By

Margrit Cruickshank

Daniel opened the front door. And there on the mat stood a monster.

It wasn't a big monster. It wasn't a huge scaly monster that breathed fire at you. Or a big hairy monster that could crush you with one paw tied behind its back. In fact, it was really quite small. It had a fat furry, green tummy, a small snouty head, big black eyes with long blue eyelashes, two stumpy scaly wings and a short fat scaly tail.

Daniel has always wanted a monster for a friend but he didn't expect it to cause so much trouble. As Charlie discovers how *not* to deal with life on Earth, Daniel and his sister Kate begin to wonder if taking in a space monster was such a good idea.

Margrit Cruickshank was shortlisted for the Irish Book Awards in 1990 and in 1992 for the Bisto Book of the Year Award.

Elf in the Head

By

Christine Nöstlinger

Anna is glad to have a friend who can hear her thoughts because she has her share of problems. Her parents live apart and she is passed between them like a parcel, mornings and overnights with Papa and afternoons with Mama.

She is getting ready for school when the elf gets into her head. He is the kind of elf that lives in heads. There is trouble in school in the form of a triangle of broken hearts: Anna, Hermann who loves her, and Peter whom Anna really loves. To resolve all these problems requires great ingenuity by Anna and lots of courage on the part of the elf.

Elf in the Head is an unusual book, funny, sad and full of nile-biting suspense.

Vienna-born Christine Nöstlinger is one of Europe's finest children's authors and winner of the Hans Christian Andersen medal for children's literature.